Outdoor Adventures!

by LYNN MASLEN KERTELL
illustrated by SUE HENDRA

SCHOLASTIC INC.

ISBN 978-1-338-81413-2

10 9 8 7 6 5 4 3 2 1   22 23 24 25 26

Printed in the United States of America 113
This edition first printing 2022

"Jack, Jack, Dad will take us on a hike today!" yells Anna.

Anna puts on sunscreen.
Jack runs to the car.

Dad brings lunch and drinks.

Jack and Anna sit in the car.
They ride and ride.

They pass the city.
They drive to the country.

"We are here!" says Dad.

Jack and Anna start up the path.

They go under trees.
They cross a stream.

"I see tracks," says Jack.
"Look! Animals!" says Anna.

11

Dad puts the picnic blanket
on the grass.
"Give that back," says Jack
to the frisky squirrel.

The sun is low.
The air cools down.
It is time to go home.

"I love hiking with you, Dad," says Anna.

"Thanks, Dad!" says Jack
as he gives Dad a hug.

The next day, Jack and Anna
want to go on another hike.

They make a picnic.
They get ready.

Mom says, "Not today, kids."

"Today you can not
go on a hike."

Jack and Anna do not drive in the car.

They do not pass the city.

They do not go into the country.

Jack says, "I know
what we can do."

Jack and Anna go in the yard.

Jack and Anna walk up the path.

They go under trees.
They cross a stream.

"Look! Animals!" says Anna.

"I see tracks," says Jack.

Anna puts their picnic
blanket on the grass.

"Give that back!" says Jack
to the frisky puppy.

The sun gets low.
The air cools down.

"Come in," calls Mom.

"We made our
say Jack and A
"Yes, you did,"
agree Mom and